BILLY AND THE MONSTERS

Monsters on a Plane

ZANNA DAVIDSON

Illustrated by
MELANIE WILLIAMSON

Reading consultant: Alison Kelly

Meet Billy...

Billy was just an ordinary boy living an ordinary life, until **ONE NIGHT** he found five **MINI MONSTERS** in his sock drawer.

Gloop

Peep

Fang-Face

Captain Snott

Trumpet

Then he saved their lives, and they swore never to leave him.

We give you the Secret-Hairy-Snot-Tooth Oath of Devotion.

We're awesome!

And fun!

And SCARY!

Are we scary? I'm not sure I'm very scary.

One thing was certain – Billy's life would never be the same **AGAIN**...

Contents

Chapter 1
Plane to Spain

Billy couldn't wait. Tomorrow he was going on vacation with his family…

…and his
MINI MONSTERS!
"We're going on a plane," said Billy. "All the way to Spain."

We're going on a plane!

A plane to Spain!

"I've never been on a plane before," said Peep, looking anxious. "Actually, I've never been on vacation before."

"I'm so excited," said Fang-Face.
"What's Spain?" asked Gloop.
"It's a country," Billy explained.

Ooh!

It looks very far away.

"It'll be **hot**," said Billy. "There'll be a pool. And we'll be near the sea."

"We've got a vacation dance," said Fang-Face. "Would you like to see it? We've been practicing."

Billy was busy worrying about his cousin… Paul. "The thing is, you see, my cousin is coming on vacation too. He's such a **goody-goody two shoes.**"

"His parents are busy working so we have to take him with us. **URGH**."

I bet he's not as cool as you, Billy.

Or as fun.

I bet he's not as awesome as me.

I hope I don't get sunburned...

"And he's a show-off," added Billy, glumly.

Everyone *loved* Paul. He was good at EVERYTHING.

Best in class

Karate champion

Best at running

Polite to grown-ups

Thank you SO much.

Spanish Dictionary

NEVER in trouble

You're so WONDERFUL, Paul.

Perfect Paul drove Billy **NUTS**.

11

"Never mind about Perfect Paul," said Fang-Face. "We're going on vacation! What could go wrong?"

"Hmm," said Billy. He couldn't help remembering all the times things *had* gone wrong.

At school...

Trumpet almost drowning in a vat of baked beans

Gloop landing on Mr. Parker's BALD PATCH

At home...

Fang-Face eating my tie

All of the monsters getting trapped in the washing machine

At the swimming pool...

Fang-Face and Captain Snott almost drowning

Gloop being sucked down the drain

And *this* time, he had to get the Mini Monsters through an airport and safely onto A PLANE without anyone seeing them.

"Okay," said Billy. "Listen carefully. I've got it all worked out."

BILLY'S BRILLIANT AIRPORT PLAN FOR MONSTERS

Part One: Check-in (STAY with me)

Baggage Drop-off

(NOT for Mini Monsters)

Part Two: Security

A) Get out of backpack

B) Get into my pocket

C) Do NOT go through X-ray machine

X-RAY

Part Three: Boarding gate (Keep hidden)

Get ready to get on the plane.

GATE 25
BOARDING NOW

Part Four: Take-off!

Mini Monsters comfy and hidden in my backpack.

"You need to stay inside my bag **AT ALL TIMES,**" said Billy, "until I tell you to come out."

The next morning, Billy got up early and put his Mini Monsters inside his bag.

"Come on, Billy," called his mom. "We're leaving."

"Is everyone ready?" asked Billy.

"Yes!" cried the Mini Monsters.

"Then hold tight," said Billy.

He raced downstairs and out the door. "Let the adventure begin…" he whispered.

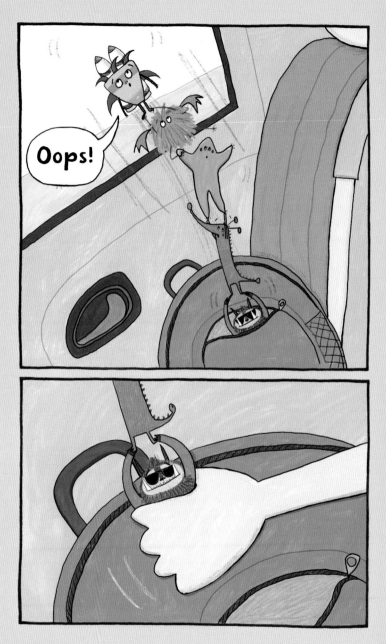

20

Chapter 2
Check-in

The airport was huge and busy.
Billy was glad the Mini Monsters
were safe inside his bag.

"Now where's Paul?" said Billy's mom. "And Aunt Sophie?"

23

"Ooh! I can see them," said Ruby. "Over there!"

MEETING POINT

"Aren't you lucky to be going on vacation with my Pauly-Wauly!" said Aunt Sophie.

Oh yes!

Oh no!

As Aunt Sophie hugged Paul goodbye, Billy tried **VERY HARD** to think nice thoughts about him.

It's not his fault he's so perfect.

It could be worse - he could have a twin and...

Um, that's it.

"Now let's find the line for the check-in desk," said Billy's dad.

"Do you know much about Spain?" asked Paul.

"**No**," said Billy.

"Then let me teach you."

The capital of Spain is Madrid.

Here we go...

The Spanish name for Spain is *España*.

Mmm. Fascinating.

"**WOW!**" said Ruby.

Billy decided not to listen to Paul any more. He was going to think about the Mini Monsters instead, and all the fun they were going to have.

"Paul might be good at everything," thought Billy. "But there's one thing he doesn't have that I do... Mini Monsters!"

Spain became a unified country in 1516.

"I'll just take a sneaky peak in my bag, to make sure they're all okay."

But as Billy unzipped the front pocket, his heart sank...

...There were two **empty** **socks.**

Gloop and Trumpet were **missing!**

Billy looked around the airport entrance hall, past the people and carts and suitcases.

Then, out of the corner of his eye, he spotted them… heading towards the baggage drop-off.

Billy tried to grab them…
But it was too late.

Billy jumped off just in time,
but Gloop and Trumpet
had **DISAPPEARED**
into the tunnel.

They were **gone**!

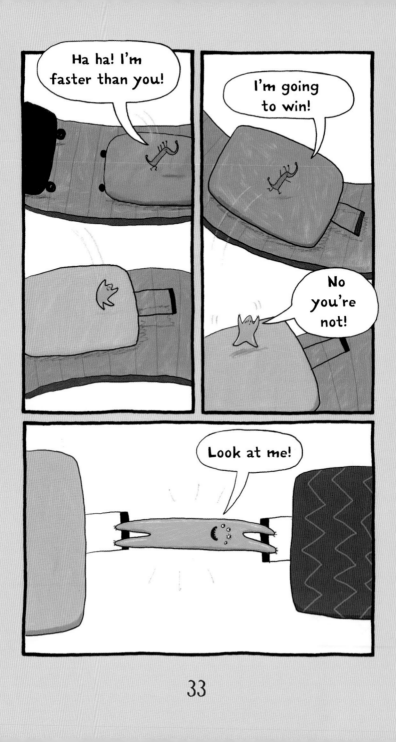

33

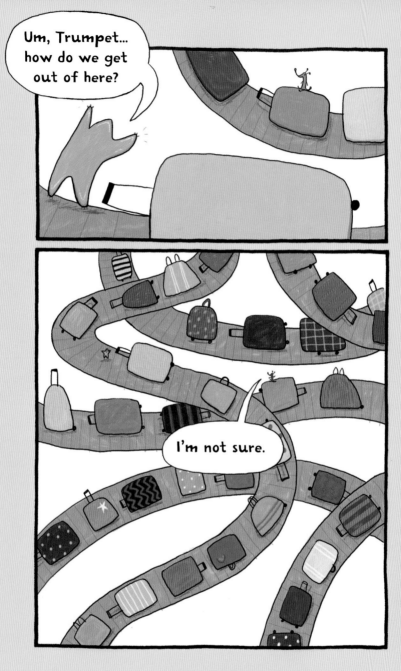

34

Chapter 3
The X-ray Machine

"What were you doing, Billy?" cried his dad. "You almost went off with the luggage!"

"Don't try that again," Billy's dad went on. "Now, next stop, **security!**"

Billy was trying to look around for Gloop and Trumpet, but his dad wouldn't let him go.

All hand
luggage
in trays.

Instead,
his dad
dragged
him towards
the security scanner.
Billy wanted to wait. He
couldn't go without Gloop and
Trumpet. But he had **no** choice.

He put
his bag in
the tray…

…and walked through the security gate.

Oh no! He'd forgotten "Part Two" of his plan.

Part Two: Security
A) Get out of backpack
B) Get into my pocket
C) Do NOT go through X-ray machine

Peep, Captain Snott and Fang-Face were in the **X-ray machine**!

"What are THOSE?" cried one of the security guards, rubbing his eyes. "Send that bag through **again!**"

Billy could only watch as his bag went through the scanner **again** and **again**.

When his bag finally came out, Billy stood over it and whispered, "ESCAPE!"

"Is this your bag?" asked one of the security guards.

Billy nodded, **nervously**.

"Would you open it, please?"

There are alive "things" in there...

Are you smuggling pets, young man?

Billy gulped. How was he going to explain **this**?

And what were they going to do to the

MINI MONSTERS

when they found them?

45

46

47

Chapter 4
Boarding

"What's this?" asked the security guard, holding up Peep.

"It's my, um,

cuddly toy,"

said Billy.

"But it was **moving**," said the other security guard. "We saw it. On the scanner!"

"It's an *electric* cuddly toy," said Billy, thinking fast.

It's from, um, Outer Mongolia. It's a very rare type of toy.

I've never seen one like that before.

Peep stood as still as he could on the table and held his breath. Billy pretended to turn him on.

49

"It's very life-like," said the
other security guard.
"Gives me the creeps.
Thought it was **ALIVE**."

I could've
sworn there
were more of
them.

"He does
have some VERY
strange toys," said Billy's dad.

The security guard scratched his head. "Well, well, well," he said, giving Peep one last look over. "Off you go then."

Billy lifted Peep, Fang-Face and Captain Snott into his bag with a smile.

"Try not to cause any more trouble," said Billy's mom.

I'm never any trouble.

"Now I just need to find Gloop and Trumpet," Billy thought.

But they weren't at the boarding gate…

…or out on the tarmac.

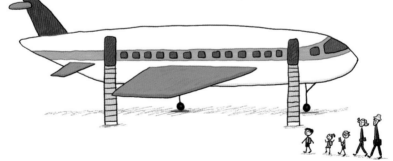

Billy walked up the steps to the plane.

"I'm going to have to leave them behind," he realized. "How will I **ever** find them again?"

"I bet Paul would never lose any Mini Monsters," thought Billy.

"I'm a **FAILURE.**"

He gazed out of the window.

Ooh, there's **Gloop**! And **Trumpet**! They're going the wrong way!

"Plane doors to close in one minute," announced the flight attendant. "I repeat, **ONE MINUTE**."

"What can I do?" thought Billy. "I can't let them close the doors. I have to get the Mini Monsters onto the plane…" He secretly lifted Fang-Face, Captain Snott and Peep out of his backpack.

Oh no!

Here's the plan…

56

57

Chapter 5
Take-off!

After a thorough search of the plane, the pilot announced, "The plane is now ready for **take-off**."

No rats or hamsters have been found on board.

Billy couldn't believe it. His plan had worked. He had all **five** Mini Monsters. Billy gave the monsters a small wave.

"Now can we do our vacation dance?" whispered Trumpet.

"Billy!" said Paul, suddenly. "I saw you. You tricked everyone with your electric toys and delayed the plane. That's SO naughty."

I'm going to have to tell a grown-up.

Don't you dare.

Billy began to think of all the ways he could stop Paul from getting to his parents and

TELLING ON HIM.

Maybe he could...

...tie Paul to his chair?

Or do something with his dictionary?

He could try hypnotizing Paul...

You saw nothing...
You have nothing to say.

...or use Trumpet's secret weapon?

But before Paul could do anything, the engines had started, and the plane began **zooming** down the runway.

Paul made a **strange noise.**

It sounded like a cross between a strangled duck and a donkey.

Then Paul clutched Billy's arm.

"Why didn't you say anything?"
"Because then I wouldn't be
perfect," wailed Paul.

The plane's engines got even
louder. It raced

faster and faster

down the runway.

Paul GROANED
and GROANED.

Take-off is the
worst! I think I
might be sick.

"Paul is a **GOODY-GOODY TWO SHOES**," thought Billy. "And he's annoyingly perfect in almost every way."

But he *IS* my cousin...

"You know my electric toys…" said Billy.

"Yes," muttered Paul.

"I think they can help you," Billy went on. "Watch this!"

Chapter 6

Vacation

"That was amazing!" said Paul.
"It was," said Billy, grinning.
"You even forgot to be scared."

Billy suddenly felt better about Paul. Nobody, he realized, was totally perfect.

"This is going to be a great vacation," he thought.

75

"Can we come to Spain next summer?" asked Captain Snott.

Billy laughed and shook his head.

"I'm **NEVER** taking you on a plane **AGAIN**," he said.

"That's fine!" said Captain Snott. "Next year we can go by **boat**."

"Maybe next year we'll stay at home," said Billy.

"Oh well," said Captain Snott, smiling. "We still have the **flight** back to look forward to…"

All about the
MINI MONSTERS

FANG-FACE

LIKES EATING:
socks, school ties,
paper, or anything
that comes his way.

SPECIAL SKILL:
has massive fangs.

SCARE FACTOR:
9/10

GLOOP

LIKES EATING: cake.

SPECIAL SKILL:
very stre-e-e-tchy.
Gloop can also swallow
his own eyeballs and
make them reappear on
any part of his body.

SCARE FACTOR:
4/10

CAPTAIN SNOTT →

LIKES EATING: boogeys.

SPECIAL SKILL:
can glow in the dark.

**SCARE
FACTOR:
5/10**

PEEP

LIKES EATING: very small flies.

SPECIAL SKILL: can fly (but
not very far, or very well).

**SCARE FACTOR:
0/10** (unless you're afraid of
small hairy things)

TRUMPET →

LIKES EATING: cheese.

SPECIAL SKILL:
amazingly powerful
cheese-powered toots.

**SCARE FACTOR:
7/10**
(taking into
account his toots)

Edited by Becky Walker
Designed by Brenda Cole
Cover design by Hannah Cobley

Digital manipulation by John Russell

First published in 2017 by Usborne Publishing Ltd., Usborne House,
83-85 Saffron Hill, London EC1N 8RT, England. www.usborne.com
Copyright © 2017 Usborne Publishing Ltd. AE